DANCE WITH ME LORD

BY DREMA R TAYLOR

DANCE WITH ME LORD
BY DREMA R TAYLOR
COPYRIGHT © 2024

DEDICATION

To My Lord and Savior, Jesus Christ,

Thanking the Holy Spirit for blessing me with the poems. Truly, it is through Him that this gift has been given to me.

To my loving husband, family, and friends who have encouraged me to publish poems.

My prayer is that in your reading time, you will be blessed and come to know the Lord, your Creator and Redeemer, as your very own. He loves you.

Romans 10:9-10 (NKJV)

9. If you confess with your mouth the Lord Jesus and believe in your heart that God has raised Him from the dead, you will be saved.

10. For with the heart one believes unto righteousness, and with the mouth confession is made unto salvation.

NOTE FROM THE AUTHOR

The Lord has truly blessed me in so many ways as the years have gone by. I feel His presence especially when the words or phrases come to me.

Sometimes one word will start the whole process, like the title "The Playground" or the first phrase "Between the glass and the ivy, a little spider dwells."

Other times, it's being involved in a situation, like sitting in front of a judge waiting for my turn because of a speeding ticket—that's when "The Day to Reckon" came into being.

I never know what will trigger a situation or when a poem will take hold. I'm so very thankful that the Holy Spirit is with me, living in me, and comforting me every day.

TABLE OF CONTENTS

FORWARD	7
THE TEST OF TIME	8
TO GAZE UPON THE FACE OF GOD	10
THE ROAD SO LONG	11
LET ME HELP YOU	13
HE WALKED AMONG US	14
JOY LIES AHEAD	16
TODAY	18
IN SEARCH OF YOU	19
GOD KNOWS	20
EYES OF GOD	21
WORDS ARE NOT GOOD ENOUGH	23
HE CARES	24
PEACE	25
THE MASTER'S GARDEN	26
HE IS	28
NEW DAY	30
PLEADING TEARS	32
HOPE	33
MY BLESSED REDEEMER	34
TO MY GOD ALONE	36
MY EVERYTHING	38
SO I THOUGHT	39
COME	41
THE WEDDING	42
THE PLAYGROUND	43
WHAT IS EASTER	45
THE MASTER FOUND ME	46
WHO AM I?	47

ECHOES	49
NEW NAME	51
FUTURE AND PAST	53
SON RAYS	54
WHAT SHALL I WEAR?	55
LITTLE SPIDER	58
WILL YOU?	61
HEAVEN'S ON A MISSION	63
WALK WITH ME	65
THE QUESTION	67
THE GRACE OF MY SALVATION	69
TEARS IN HEAVEN	71
SAYING GOODBYE	72
THE DAY TO RECKON	74
DANCE WITH ME LORD	76
TEA PARTY FRIENDS	78
IT'S BEEN A WHILE	80
THE STRUGGLE	82
SCARS	84
STANDING ON THE EDGE	86
WISHING WELLS AND FAIRY TALES	88
HEAVEN'S HEARTBEAT	90
HEAVEN'S TIMEPIECE	92
EVIL'S PLAN	94
ROBIN	96

FORWARD

I have had the great pleasure of serving as one of Drema Taylor's pastors at Three Rivers Church. Drema began sharing her poems with me at church when she found out that I was an educator. I could immediately see that there was something special about her arrangement of words.

In *Heaven's Heartbeat*, she wrote the line, "His love for His creation nailed Him to the tree that He created be," and it resonated in my heart. What resonated was not the words or the author but the Author of Life—Jesus Christ.

Drema loves the Lord and loves using her talents to express, through poetry, the deep and sincere love she has for her Lord and Savior, Jesus Christ. I know these poems will captivate you, bless you, and draw you closer to Jesus.

Mark Lang

THE TEST OF TIME

Today I stand upon this shore; this time, this day, will be no more.

Tomorrow rests upon the crest, rolling in so hard, so fast,

melding with the breaking waves, disappearing within my gaze.

Life passes swiftly, each wave lapping after the last, rolling out again into oblivion.

The waves have crashed so hard and fast. Here I stand, a half-century past. Time has been stolen.

I can recall the past, a babe upon a lap, cradled in loving arms.

It feels like yesterday those loving arms enveloped me.

As I gazed upon the face of the one who bore me.

Time has now claimed that beloved one, out of my sight, beyond my grasp. She now sits, encircled by the light.

I will meet her once again when my life comes to the end, when my time has ebbed away

with my final breath, I will say, "Lord Jesus, take me home."

At the feet of God above, I will reunite with all those I love, but most of all, at last, no more minutes will pass; time will stand still.

Forevermore, I will be with the one who died for me. I will sing praises to His name with each breath I draw, as I gaze lovingly into the face of God.

Drema R Taylor
September 24, 1999

TO GAZE UPON THE FACE OF GOD

I can't fathom when time will be no more, and I cross over to the other shore,
Beyond the crystal sea.

All creation at my feet - the earth, the sky, the stars, each feat,
By the artist's brush, no mortal could decree.

The brilliance of a sunset, or innocence in a child's eyes, so set,
The warmth of your husband's embrace, so free.

The sweetness of your baby's smile, a precious mile,
With all God's gifts, for us to taste, to smell, to see.

I can't envision how beautiful the Face of God must truly be.

Drema R Taylor
September 24, 1999

THE ROAD SO LONG

There it lies before me as I look and gaze beyond,
The long, lonesome highway of lives.

Filled with snares that ever bind,
I thought life would be different.

Time has proven right, the heart of man is wicked,
Evil in God's sight.

Can you see the meaning, the hurt, the pain?
I see humans inflicting upon each other, living desperately.

I see the faces daily, looking here and there,
Trying to recover from lives of disdain, despair.

My heart cries out for them to see what I have found,
My road is so full of grace, my head will wear a crown.

For my Savior has found me on that road I spoke about,
I was so torn and tattered, but He sought me out.

He loved even before I knew Him and thought me worth His while,
He gave me a crown and now calls me His child.

That road was long and lonely for my Savior,
The people turned their backs, they yelled, they cursed, they spat on Him,
But 'He only loved them back'.

He made that long trip up THAT ROAD, THAT DAY.
He was so torn and tattered, but on that road He stayed.

You see, the trip was not easy, for alone He would go:
Would He find you there in life's ebb and flow?

Upon the cross, He hung, so full of despair,
He cried out, "Father, forgive them, you know how much I care."

God in His great mercy, sacrificed His Son,
Only because He loves us, and no other one.

God can call up sticks and stones to sing praises to His name,
But He wants only you, for only you He came.

Drema R Taylor
September 25, 1999

LET ME HELP YOU

Here, let me help you; let me show you the way.
Let me tell you of a person that you will meet one day.

That person is courageous and loyal to a fault.
A lie has never passed His lips; truth He always sought.

He's always been honest, never stolen a thing.
He'll fight your battles, take the blame life may bring.

He'll be your shield and your doctor too;
He'll feed and clothe you, if you want him to.

He'll give you strength in your darkest hour;
He'll walk beside you, give you power.

He'll be with you in the valley or on the mountaintop;
He'll guide you through the sands of time, without a stop.

He'll never cause you doubt; His courage shines bright.
The person I speak of is the Son of Light.

As you gaze upon the cross and see His scarred hands,
He says, "I've loved you this much; won't you let me in?"

Do yourself a favor; open up that door.
Let Him come into your life and live forevermore.

Drema R Taylor
September 29, 1999

HE WALKED AMONG US

He came to Earth, a lowly man, born to a family poor.
He walked the earth to teach God's love, sharing truth with all.

Yet they would not listen, they would not heed the call.

Deaf ears remained shut, hard hearts refused to bend,
But still, he walked on, teaching truth to every friend.

The final days approached, he knew the pain too well,
The weight of sin upon him, a burden hard to quell.

He cried out in the garden, "Father, give me strength,
Your will be done, not mine," This body is human, my sprit divine.

Great drops of blood he sweated, as he poured out his heart,
Upon his knees my savior prayed, the Father did impart,
The strength needed for the deed, to fulfill his part.

"King of the Jews," they called him, yet they did not understand,
He was the King, the Son of Man, fulfilling God's plan.

Upon Calvary's hill, the wooden cross was hung,
Darkness covered the land, as the Father turned away from his son.

The earth did shake, the veil was torn, truly he was the Son of God,
They cried out, "To late, he didn't hear them, he was on his way."

Into the depths of the earth, to set the captives free,
"Oh death, where is your sting? Oh grave, your victory?"

Three days later, the tomb lay empty where he was laid to rest,
He appeared before them, saying, "Come, see, test."
Did I not tell you what I had to do?

Now I'm going to the Father, but you'll never be alone,
We send you the Holy Spirit, to guide you, to lead you home.

How can you not accept his love, freely given,
To cleanse you from your sins, and welcome you to heaven?

Drema R Taylor
September 29, 1999

JOY LIES AHEAD

When I went to church as a child,
I heard people singing and praising God. I didn't know,
couldn't figure it out,
What all the joyous noise was about.

"What are they talking about, being saved from your sins?
What's that anyway?" I didn't understand.

Then they told me a story of how Jesus died.
"He was crucified," they said, "between two others who had
broken the law."

I asked, "What did He do? Was He to blame too?"
"Oh no, my dear," they said, "He was innocent as a lamb.
But God loved us so much, He had to find a way
To cleanse us and wash our sins away."

Then the Great Creator said He had a plan.
He would come to earth and live as a man,
So God came to earth to set our spirits free,
To give us life for eternity.

Joy lies ahead, with empty roads behind,
I have put my trust in the one who is divine.
As I look into the future, as far as I can see,
I see that mighty river flowing into the crystal sea.

The streets of gold I'll tread upon,

As I wonder in awe of all the beauty made by the hand of God.

Drema R Taylor
October 16, 1999

TODAY

Today I've sat and spent some time with the Lord that I call mine.
I've read His word, opened my heart, with His spirit He did impart
Strength I needed for this day, to keep me on the narrow way.

In His word, I search for wisdom and truth,
Knowing I'll find guidance for this life, uncouth.

I read between the covers, the greatest story ever told,
Of a Savior who really loves me, and one day I'll walk His streets of gold.

Drema R Taylor
December, 1999

IN SEARCH OF YOU

Lord, I came to your house today,
I bowed my head and prayed.
I lifted my voice in sweet song,
And raised my hands to you, so strong.

My heart was full of love,
My eyes gazed to heaven above.
All my thoughts rested on you,
You're the reason I came through.

I came to your table, not to feast,
But to taste the bread and wine, the least.

You told us to do these things,
To keep you fresh in our hearts and springs.

I searched my heart for sin or darkness,
You shone your light, so relentless.

That I could see nothing,
Standing between you and me.

I took the bread and dipped the wine,
Placed it in this body of mine.
I felt the warmth of your sweet love,
I'm so glad that I am loved by my Lord God above.

Drema R Taylor
December, 1999

GOD KNOWS

Birds fly across the sky, as clouds drift gently past,
Warm summer breezes tousle my hair, I feel free at last.

Pressures surround me on every side, that daily living brings,
Yet as I turn to my God, my heart begins to sing.

I pray, and my Father listens with an attentive ear,
Just as my earthly father did, with love so clear.

My God, My Father, knows all that weighs on me,
With loving care, He says, "Dear child, let me see."

Sometimes what you ask of me is not what I can give,
And when I say no, you may think I don't care, but believe:

I hear all you ask, but sometimes what you want is not what's best,
On that, I must pass, to ensure you're truly blessed.

Problems come and go, they're all a part of living,
Isn't it comforting to know God reigns in Heaven.

Drema R Taylor
November, 1999

EYES OF GOD

When God gazes upon me, what does He see? What does He see?
Does He find a heart clean and pure, or one cold and cruel?

Does He perceive a heart blessed by Him, or one burdened with sin?
Is there light illuminating every part, or darkness casting its mark?

What does He see when He looks at me? Does He see a troubled soul,
Tossed by the winds, out of control?

Or someone who is sure and will endure?

When the eyes of God behold me, He sees me as I am,
Whether weathered and worn or in grandeur stand.

He sees a soul filled with love, reaching for heavenly goals,
Someone who knows His healing touch, one who's been to the throne of grace.

When He checks on me, as He often does, to see if I need His guiding hand,
Or just a measure of His boundless love.

When the eyes of God survey me, He sees me as I am.

He recognizes that I've been redeemed, bought with the price of His Lamb.

When I cry out His name, He answers, "Here I am."
When God looks at me, He sees me as I am.

Drema R Taylor
January 18, 2000

WORDS ARE NOT GOOD ENOUGH

Words are not good enough to sing praises to my King.
They roll off my lips as I close my eyes and sing.

My spirit swells within my breast,
taken to a place where Alleluias ring,
standing as my spirit sings.

Before your throne I am, though I can't see your face.
Hidden by your Glory and the clouds that fill the space.

Your awesome power electrifies the air,
my spirit on its face, weeping and praising God.

Overwhelmed, my heart is full of love,
back to earth to finish the song I had just begun.

Words are not enough to sing praises to your name,
let Alleluias and Hosannas ring.

Renewed is my soul, I'll visit you again,
closing my eyes to come to you, my Savior, King, and friend.

Drema R Taylor
April 09, 2000

HE CARES

As I walked the ocean's shores,
I beheld quite a sight.
Many sea gulls soared,
screeching with delight.

Facing the ocean waves,
seeking sustenance for the day,
it reminded me in a gentle way.

As God cares for the birds of the air,
Aren't we so much better?
He purchased us at a price so high,
it brought tears to Heaven's eyes.

Drema R Taylor
Jan 15, 2000

PEACE

When I was lost and so alone, my life filled with despair,
You came to me with open arms, and said,
"My child, come here."

I ran to you, fell on my face, found grace and mercy there.
You picked me up, you set me free, my burdens now you bear.

You gave me hope, you gave me strength,
On bended knee I came, my soul cried out to you,
I'll never be the same.

On bended knee I come, you will see me through,
From this life to the next, I am coming to you.

Drema R Taylor
December 03, 2003

THE MASTER'S GARDEN

I met the Master Gardener today,
As I wandered down the lane.
"Master Gardener," I said,
"Could you share with me your plan?"

Well, today I'm planting Kindness,
And I'll watch it as it grows.
It'll spread across the land,
And emit a heavenly glow.

Kindness, a special fruit,
It grows, it spreads, takes root,
And changes the hearts of man,
If they allow it to.

With Kindness comes goodness,
They travel hand in hand.
Oh, did I mention gentleness?
It's in the perfect plan.

Yesterday, I planted Love and Peace.
It was delightful to see,
All those people smile,
As they realized Joy was spread for miles.

Faithfulness, it's thriving well,
Though sometimes self-control may dwindle.

The most challenging, forgiveness,
As I toil in the garden, tending and watering.

Lives are changed, hearts are healed,
Life can go on tenfold,
When forgiveness finally takes hold.

Longsuffering, another challenging one,
But breakthrough will surely come.

Come, let me prune you,
Cut out all that doesn't belong.
Come, let me love you,
And watch you grow strong.

Drema R Taylor
March 03, 2003

HE IS

There is a place that I go
When my soul is in distress.
When I go on bended knees,
He draws me to His breast.

He is so close, just a prayer away.
He listens to everything I say.

He is, He is my Savior.

He lets me know that I am loved,
And keeps me close by Him.
Here I feel so secure,
My soul is safe with Him.

Surrounded by the arms of God,
In Him I am so blessed.
He keeps me through my darkest hour,
In Him I find my rest.

He is so close, just a prayer away.
He listens to everything I say.

He is, He is my Savior.

There is such perfect peace,
A calming of my soul.

He lifts me up and lets me know
That He is in control.

Come let Him hold you tight
And comfort you the same.
Just meet Him there on bended knee,
And call upon His name.

He is so close, just a prayer away.
He listens to everything you say.

He is, He is our Savior.

Drema R Taylor
June 10, 2003

NEW DAY

New every morning is the promise from above,
With every dawn, He fills my heart with love.

I think of Him and joy floods my soul,
I trusted Him and He made me whole.

His eyes are always watching,
His ears, they always hear,
His arms are ever ready
To encircle me with care.

When hurts fill my heart and sorrow tears my soul,
He is there to comfort and console.

I make Him laugh when I am joyful,
He smiles at the silly things I do.

When I sing my songs of love to Him,
It truly warms Him too.

I am His creation; He made me this way,
And after shaping me, He threw the mold away.

For we are all different, not one the same,
Unique beings, He calls us by our name.

He had plans for us long before
We saw the light of day.
In God's master plan, we each have a part,

Precious in His sight, He holds us in His heart.

He wants you to know He loves you, but
There's something you must do,
Open up your heart to Him,
He will see you through.

Drema R Taylor
December 03, 2003

PLEADING TEARS

I come to You, pleading through a veil of tears,
For those who have wasted their time, their years.

Today they draw their last breath,
Standing at time's edge, facing death.
Will they never see Your face? Father,
When eternity lies within Your hands,
While time, a mere construct for man,
Measured by each grain of sand
In a glass called time and space?

Father, please stop the time for them,
Grant one last chance
To behold Your Mercy and Grace.

Eternity, cold and dark, devoid of peace,
Echoes with tortured souls, never to cease.
Begging and pleading, unheard cries,
Their terror bound to them, never to die.

Endless darkness, endless plight,
Father, have mercy,
Grant them one last light,
To call upon Your name, to live anew,
In Your Mercy, in Your amazing Grace.

Drema R Taylor
June 15, 2005

HOPE

Alone, my ship sat on the sea,
No wind to carry me.

My sails were torn,
My rudder broke,
And here I am, barely afloat.

The seas they rage, I'm tossed about,
Lost in despair, no way out.

From up above, the light shone through,
It filled me with a love so true.

My sails are fixed, my rudder sure,
My destination now secure.

Though seas may rage and winds may blow,
I know who's in control, I know.

The Creator of land and sea,
Also created and loves me.

He loved me then, He loves me still,
I live now to do His will.

Drema R Taylor
March 30, 2004

MY BLESSED REDEEMER

Blessed Redeemer, lover of my soul,
You saved me, cleansed me, and made me whole.

Lost, You found me; sick from sin,
You touched my heart, brought peace within.

When sorrow overwhelms,
I turn my eyes to You.
You comfort, protect, and see me through.

You are my firm foundation,
The rock on which I stand.
All else around me is sinking sand.

Keep your eyes on Jesus,
Who paid the price for you.
He alone is worthy, faithful and true.

I sing to You each morning,
Think of You throughout the day.

One day, You will call my name,
I will see Your face, no more to stray.

My Blessed Redeemer,
I will sing of Your amazing grace.

Heaven's gates will open wide,

I will be home at last, by Your side.

Drema R Taylor
March 25, 2005

TO MY GOD ALONE

I praise You in the morning light,
At noon and in the evening's sight,
And through the silent hours of night,
My praise to You takes flight.

In every circumstance,
Beyond my control's expanse,
With holy hands, I raise,
My worship to Your throne ablaze.

You are my Father, God of eternity,
Creator of all, my divine fraternity.
I am Yours, Yours alone,
Existence finds purpose at Your throne.

I'm here for Your pleasure,
What other purpose could there be?
But to love and trust You
Through all eternity.

You bought me with a price so high,
You gave Your best for me.
Here I stand before Your grace,
Praising Your name, seeking Your face.

One day You will call me,
I will see You face to face,
I will join all heaven's angels,

To sing "Amazing Grace."

Holy, Holy, Holy,
To You, my God alone.
Holy, Holy, Holy,
Before Your throne, I am Your own.

Drema R Taylor
April 07, 2005

MY EVERYTHING

When I close my eyes,
I see your face,
Falling on my knees,
Surrounded by your grace.

In the palm of your hand,
You hold me tight,
In all that I am,
I find my light.

You give me love,
You give me peace,
You provide all,
My soul's release.

You're my Lord,
My soon-coming King,
In every breath,
You are my everything.

Drema R Taylor
August 01, 2006

SO I THOUGHT

Young and so carefree when you first came to me.
Walking on the mountain top,
I did not heed your voice,
Life was good, or so I thought.

The Holy One reaching out for me,
Calling my name, you a mystery.

Running aimlessly, here and there,
I did not have a care.
Life was good, or so I thought.

Time passed; some things changed.
My life has been rearranged.
Deep in the valley with lots of pain,
Life brought me to my knees.

You are the Holy one reaching out for me,
Calling my name.

I heard you voice that day,
So soft and sweet, As I fell at your feet.

You gave me life, you put breath in me
You opened my eyes so I could see.
I have it all, every part; eternal life you did impart.
Heaven will be my home. I am no longer alone.

The Holy One, watching over me,
Calling my name, *NO LONGER A MYSTERY*.

Drema R Taylor
September 27, 2019

COME

Come to me, He calls; I look upon His face.
Come to my shelter, and there you find grace.

Come, let me hold you, find your rest,
In my love, you'll be blessed.

With hands raised high, heart at His throne,
I worship Him, and Him alone.

Majesty and everlasting God,
You gave me life, with love untrod.

Breathed into me Your sacred breath,
Called me by name, saved from death.

Come to God, He calls to you,
Freedom and life, He will imbue.

Drema R Taylor
September 26, 2019

THE WEDDING

I'm going to a wedding, my gown sparkling white,
Surrounded by the other souls so bright.
My Bridegroom, He is coming, I feel Him drawing near,
Excitement builds, anticipation clear.

The wedding party is growing larger every day,
We all feel the excitement as we watch and pray.
It will be so grand, millions will be there,
Celebrating with our Bridegroom, we won't have a care.

How glorious that day will be when my Bridegroom comes for me.
I hear the shout, He's coming, can't you see?

He called me by my name, His voice clear and bright,
We'll all rejoice in His light.

Blessed are those who are called to the Marriage Supper of the Lamb, for we are the Bride of Christ. He has come to claim us as His own.
Revelation 19:7-9

Time will then be gone. I will forever be with the One who died for me.

Drema R Taylor
March, 2020

THE PLAYGROUND

The devil has a playground, nestled in the minds of man.
He makes things feel so right; it's a sinful plan.

All feels good for a moment, all feels right with the world.
Fame and fortune beckon you, promising delight.

Just as he requires the payment, it doesn't seem so bad,
A little piece of you—that's all he asks.

As the years have passed, he has almost your whole.
There's not a lot left of you. You are out of control.

Darkness creeps, loneliness deepens under his deceitful spell.
He claims you as his, a captive of his hell.

So dark and lonely where you're at.
He smiles in glee and tips his hat,
Says you are mine and mine alone, nothing you can do.

Lost and desperate, you raise your eyes to heaven above,
Begging for mercy, seeking His love.

God, in His grace, extends His hand,
shows you the love that's been there, waiting, planned.

The Son who died upon the cross awaits you with His grace,
To cleanse, to heal, to fill your soul's empty space.

The Lamb gave His life to cleanse and make you whole.
Joy now floods your soul.

The playground in your mind transformed by His embrace,
Now belonging to Christ, in His love and grace.

Drema R Taylor
March 22, 2020

WHAT IS EASTER

Easter isn't bunnies or chickies in view,
It's about the one who died for you.

Easter isn't pretty eggs, colors arrayed,
It's about the tomb where He laid.

Easter is not about baskets of candy, surprises inside,
Easter is about the One who sacrificed and died.

Easter isn't bonnets with flowers to adorn,
It's about forgiveness, love reborn.

Easter is not about going to church once a year,
Easter is about loving Him, holding Him dear.

Easter is about God's power displayed,
Raising Him from death's dark shade.

Easter is about His boundless love shed,
And the gift of life for all who have bled.

Easter is about the gift He gave to you,
Eternal life, if you ask Him to.

Drema R Taylor
April 07, 2020

THE MASTER FOUND ME

I have been redeemed, I have been forgiven.
I am a child of God, a child of Heaven.

The Master found me when I was lost,
Claimed me as His own, from the cross.

I've brought Him heartache, brought Him pain,
Yet He watched over me, never in vain.

Patiently He waited as life brought me to my knees,
Doubting His love for someone like me.

He forgave my sins, made me whole,
Now I know the depths of His soul.

I have been redeemed, I have been forgiven.
I am a child of God, a child of Heaven.

One glorious day, I'll meet the One who died for me,
Living with Him through eternity.

A child of God, in His embrace,
In Heaven's light, I find my place.

I am a child of God, a child of Heaven.

Drema R Taylor
May 24, 2020

WHO AM I?

There's a question in my mind,
Who am I? Who am I?

Running constantly, lost in doubt,
In fear, with no way out.

Who am I? Who am I?

Some days seem impossible to tread,
Down a road where all else has fled.
Who am I?

Life's mysteries hard to comprehend,
Whipped by the wind, to my knees I bend.
Crying out to the One who formed me,
Who am I?

Dead in sin, I called out His name,
Heartache screaming, "Please, come tame."
Who am I?

Once lost, now I'm found,
I know who I am, my soul's sound.

Called redeemed and justified,
Forgiven for my sins, I now abide.

I am called a child of God.
I am loved by Him, that's who I am,
His child is who.... I..... am.....

Written as a song *Drema R Taylor*
May 24, 2020

ECHOES

I hear the echoes in my mind,
A distant place, a lost time.

I was lost and all alone,
Forgetting who I am, unknown.

Standing there, in solitude,
Painful memories, misconstrued.

My heart cries out, in silent plea,
I run, I hide, searching to be free.

Searching for hope, a voice I hear,
Whispering softly, drawing near.

"Come to me," it gently calls,
Rest in my embrace, in my halls.

Wrapped in love, find happiness,
In my arms, find true blessedness.

Cast your cares upon my grace,
I'll mend your heart, in this space.

Through eternity, I'll keep you near,
My forgiveness, forever sincere.

Echoes linger in my mind,
But in His love, solace I find.

Drema R Taylor
September 27, 2020

NEW NAME

I have a new name I haven't heard before.
On the day I was placed beneath a beating heart,
One cell came to be; I was called that name
Right then and there, from the very start.

On the day of birth, my mother called to me.
Her voice was sweet, like a melody.
I smiled at her, and she smiled back at me,
Calling me the name she chose lovingly.

My whole life, that is who I have been,
Until I draw my last breath and my journey ends.

I know I have a new name.
I will hear it called by the One who created me.
He watched me grow and guided my way.
One day, I will behold His glory and grace.

That beautiful name I was given is now
Recorded in the Book of Life.
It was placed there when I gave my life to Christ.
The angels' harps played a heavenly sound,
On that joyous day, my soul was found.

Drema R Taylor
September 26, 2020

Rev 2:17
That beautiful name that I was given is now recorded in the Book of Life; it was placed there the day I gave my life to Christ. The angels' harps were playing; they had a heavenly sound, that joyous day my soul was found.

Rev 19:16
His name is the Word of God. Lord of Lords, King of Kings, are titles that He's known. It will be a glorious day there before His throne. He is my blessed Redeemer, the Savior of my soul.

FUTURE AND PAST

Lord, You knocked upon my heart's door today.
I opened the door for You.
Come in, Lord, and stay with me, and be my Redeemer too.

Lord, my heart is cluttered with things from my past.
Look deep within and shine Your light.
Root out everything that is unacceptable and purge it
From the deepest part of my heart.

Lord, consume every part of me—the good and the bad.
Cleanse me, Lord, and make me new.

Living in the present, where future and past collide,
Sometimes I am confused, struggling inside.
Come and make me whole, fill me with Your love untold.
Give me rest and comfort for my soul.

Standing amazed at Your glory and grace,
Your deep, abiding love draws me near.
Keep me in Your power, hold me in Your hand,
Your love surrounding me again.

Drema R Taylor
October 27, 2020

SON RAYS

Tears fall in the still of night.
Cascades of sorrow in my plight.
Tears of joy, tears of pain,
Tears, they fall like rain.

Rays of sunshine through the tears of pain.
Life, oh life, continues its refrain.

Are they forgotten? Were they ever known?
Did you see them? Were their hearts made of stone?
Life is filled with stories, small and grand,
Sunshine so bright, nothing hidden in the light.

Shining through to the forest floor,
The rays bring life, restoring more.

Our Savior is the Son, and His rays are the ones,
Bringing life to our souls, granting eternal life evermore.

Drema R Taylor
October 27, 2020

WHAT SHALL I WEAR?

Going to my closet,
Looking there, trying to find
Something to wear.

I search through the racks
Of all the clothes I have.
I search and search to no avail;
Nothing fits together well.

I have another set of clothes no human eye can see;
I wear this set of clothes.
They protect me from the unseen world
That surrounds you and me.

My heavenly closet is hidden,
No one knows it's there.
My closet door will open as I turn the golden key of prayer.

My clothing on wooden hangers
Hang there; they do not stand.
My heavenly coverings need no racks;
They simply suspend.

My helmet of salvation, I wear, is not made
By mortal man; it is covered by the blood of
Christ, my dear Lord, instead.

The shoes in my closet are not needed to walk
On sand; I walk barefoot on the water
Because Jesus holds my hand.

My special shoes are given
To spread the light to all the world.
God loves you now and evermore.

The belt around my waist, the sash that I wear,
Is held there by the scarlet threads
In His body He bears.

I have a shiny breastplate,
It guards my heart and covers me in righteousness
My Lord imparts.

Taking up my shield of faith,
Keeps me from the fiery darts
The enemy daily throws my way.

I have a mighty sword; it's of the Spirit made,
It is called the *Word of God*.
It is so powerful the enemy has to flee;
It can't stand in the presence of the Almighty.

My prayer is my lifeline;
I speak to my Lord every day.
He keeps me on the narrow way.

I have quite a wardrobe that I wear every day.

I am armed for battle on my life's highway.

Although I am dressed as oddly as can be,
My battle gear is on just right;
It's just that you can't see.

Drema and Robert Taylor
January 20, 2021

LITTLE SPIDER

Between the glass and ivy,
A little spider dwells.
He builds all his waking hours
For a home to make.

He toils and works, spinning his web,
A very intricate design.
He knows just what he's doing,
Keeps every move in mind.

He keeps an eye on his web,
In case a visitor comes by.
His web he will not share; if something else gets in, then his lunch they will make.

Such a tiny thing, this little spider is,
Living in a world of giants,
Great care he must take.

If he shows himself to the world,
Then he may be doomed instead.

For such is the world we live in,
There are giants around.

As we build our homes and lives,
With great care we must take.

For the enemy lurks in the shadows,
Sometimes in the form of a snake.

Things are not always as simple
As they should be.
Sin creeps in; it is hidden,
And we can't see.

A little white lie, a bigger lie,
A wandering eye; then sin will be exposed.

Before you can figure out how
This far you have come,
You are deep within the throes of sin,
You need to be set free.

There is hope for redemption,
A Savior to rescue you
From the life of sin you've been caught up in.
When your life is in tatters with lots of missing parts,
Ask Him to pick you, forgive you, give you a fresh start.

Your heart will be free to worship Him,
As you were made to do.
Because "dear friend," He paid a very dear price,
Out of love for you.

This life will continue and sometimes
It might get hard, but on the other side
Of this life, you will find your resting place,

Living with and loving our Savior.

The little spider spins his web, works hard all day long.
One day his life will end; another will take his place.
Life in the spider web will go on, a new generation to take.

Drema and Robert Taylor
January 25, 2021

WILL YOU?

There are things you must do.
Will you believe He has redeemed your soul?
Will you believe He has made you whole?

Will you give up your self-control?
Will you let Him in,
Let Him be Lord of all?

Come to Him with a yearning heart, as a child.
He imparts all the innocence reconciled.
He forgives you of your sin.

These things of great importance,
They will save your soul and set you free.

Are your eyes searching the sky?
Is your heart crying out?
How much longer will it be?
Before You come for me?

He is coming to get His Bride.
Are you going to be ready or be surprised?
That you are left behind?

Arrayed in all His glory bright,
Our Bridegroom, a wondrous sight.
We will shine like stars above,

Melting within His amazing love.

Will you be ready?
Will you?

Drema R Taylor
February 14, 2021

HEAVEN'S ON A MISSION

Heaven's on a mission to reclaim the souls of men.
You see, it won't be easy—it's been a long time since Adam sinned.

The great deceiver found Eve in the garden,
Told her she could be more like God and less like man.
That's where sin began!

A loving Savior came to earth in the form of a man.
He did what He had to do to reclaim those souls that had been stolen, living in God's plan.

He was nailed to a cross, buried, rose again to set the captive free. Death, where is your sting?
Grave, where is your victory?

Our righteous warrior will come back to claim all that is His.
The evil one thought he had won on the day he deceived.

The roaring Lion of Judah has proved him wrong.
The roaring Lion will come and claim His throne.

God's Lamb has paid the price for all souls who come freely to Him.
Oh Mighty Warrior, you are fierce to behold.
No eye has seen, no tongue can tell, the power you control.

The day is fast approaching when everything will change,
When that trumpet sounds and the clouds will split. His fury
will rain upon the evil one and all who don't believe.

Heaven has a mission. The great victory has been won.
We are waiting now for our Lord's return.

We will forever be with God our Father and His Son,
Our Lord Jesus Christ, for all eternity.

Drema R Taylor
March 24, 2021

WALK WITH ME

Come walk with me, hold my hand,
Keep me close, help me understand.
Where is my life going, remind me where I have been?

As a child, I looked into my father's face,
His loving eyes upon me, he said, "Come,
Walk with me, hold my hand."

Down the lane we walked, I felt safe, his hand in mine,
We talked and laughed, our time divine.

I've known you for so long, I've failed you in many ways,
Yet you have always stayed on the path where I sometimes strayed.
You stop and beckon with your outstretched hand,

Come walk with me, come hold my hand.

I reached for you, looked into your face,
Saw love in YOUR EYES, felt it in your embrace.

"Come walk with me," You beckon, showing love so grand,
You reach out your scarred, nail-marked hands.
You say, "Come walk with me, let me hold your hand."

I knew you before you were formed, I watched you grow,
With the father I gave you, down that lane you'd go.

I smiled seeing the love he had for you.

On the other side of your father, I held his hand,
Together we walked down that lane, laughter filled the land.

He still walks with me on streets of gold,
He held my hand until life's tale was told.

Come walk with Me, come hold my hand,
Until this life ends and your new life begins.

Drema R Taylor
April 23, 2021

THE QUESTION

See the people running there, they do not have a care,
Going this way and that, living their daily lives,
Much like in Noah's day, people ran and played.

Messages preached to them, "Look, your life's full of sin,
Come repent, know Him."

God in heaven can't look on sin, He'll turn His back on you,
For not listening to Him.

They ran here and there, they did not have a care,
Until drops of rain began to fall,
And the flood consumed them all.

They screamed and cried, "Let us in,"
But to no avail, they died in their sin.

The door was shut, their fate was sealed.

For such as we live in this day, time will no longer delay.
One day soon, the rain of pain will fall on all those who said
no.
They will recall the day and time it was asked of them.

"Do you know Jesus? Do you live in sin?"

"But I am a good person," you would say,

"I have been moral in every way.
My goodness sparkles and shines through everything I do.
I know when I die, God will see me as I do."

Do you think works alone will suffice?
No, sorry to say, there is not enough you can do to be cleansed and made anew.

The only way to reconcile is to call on Jesus before you die.
Call on Him and be made whole,
He will make you whiter than snow.

God gave His very best for you,
His only Son bled and died for you.
He alone can make you whole.

Only through Him will you see the Father's face,
We will spend eternity praising the Father, His Son, and the Holy Spirit, the guiding one.

So I ask you once again, do you know Jesus?
But the better question is, does Jesus know you?

Are you free from sin? Are you blessed and cleansed by Him?

Drema R Taylor
November 16, 2021

THE GRACE OF MY SALVATION

The grace of my salvation has come to earth,
His grace and mercy reign forever in eternity.

His love, so warm and deep,
The Creator has come to earth, to dwell in our skin.

To feel the pain that we suffer, to bless us within,
The Healer has come to earth.

In His body, He bears the scars for all eternity,
To show us how much He cares.

The Sustainer of life has come to earth,
To free us from our sin, to feel the grief we share, to be loved by Him.

The redeemer of my soul has paid the price for me,
His blood on the ground that He created to be.

For He knew He must pay a price to free us from our sins,
The wooden Cross on which He hung, prepared by Him before time began.

His grace and mercy cover me, sustain me in His love,
I live now through all eternity, my praises now I give.

The Creator of earth, Redeemer of my soul,

Healer of my heart, He has made me whole!

Drema R Taylor
November 17, 2021

TEARS IN HEAVEN

Father weeps over His creation,
So soon torn away from the life He wished they had known.

Doctors, lawyers, inventors,
Presidents and kings.

They could have changed the world,
Brought so much good within their wings.

Tears in Heaven flow over
All the lives that are lost.

His loved ones are gone,
Torn from streets, classrooms,
And wombs where safety was sought, but in vain.

Evil finds its way to destroy, steal, and kill,
We mourn their loss. It pains to know they're gone,
No laughter heard, no smiles seen,
No chance to grow into who they could have been.

To bless the world, to fulfill their purpose,
As the wonderful people God intended them to be.

Drema R Taylor
May 25, 2022

SAYING GOODBYE

Saying goodbye is never easy,
Sometimes the hardest thing you will ever do.

As you sit and ponder your life,
And what's coming next for you.

So many games have been played,
And brought much joy your way.

With shining eyes and great big smiles,
Life has been truly good.

Now, time to ponder once again,
As time marches on and years disappear,

Through all the sadness and all the tears,
One thing remains the same.

The love I have for the reason I live,
Christ Jesus is His name.

One day He will call me, I will see His face,
And all who wait in His glory and grace.

Saying goodbye is never easy,
But if you know where they go,

Makes it worth the pain,

For I will see you all again,

Those who trusted in our Savior,
Held Him in their hearts.

A grand homecoming it will be,
Loving and praising our Savior,

For all eternity.

Saying goodbye is never easy,
Until we meet again.

Drema R Taylor
January 02, 2023

THE DAY TO RECKON

Standing before the judge can be a dreadful thing,
Knowing the laws you have broken.
Life will never be the same.

Thinking back, you see how your life has been,
All the sins committed, your world in a spin.

Years gone by, wasted tears shed.
Are you sorry for them? Are you filled with dread?

The judge is sitting on His throne, robed in majesty,
He alone knows your past; all the deeds you've done
Are written in the book that He has read.

The crimes you've committed,
The lies you've told, things you are guilty of.
He looks at your face. His eyes pierce your soul.
You can't escape His gaze,
There's no place to run, no place to hide.
You're standing there alone.

A commotion to your right, and the judge looks away,
He sees a commanding figure come into His presence
With a smile on His face.

He starts to speak on my behalf:
Your Honor, if I may bring evidence to his defense

And show you a different way.

This man is innocent of the charges,
I have paid the price.
He came to me on bended knee and gave me his life.

The evidence before you I'm entering into the records of the court.
The payment has been made, I'm happy to report.

Here are my nail-scarred hands and feet,
My crown of thorns upon my head,
As I'm standing before you in my resurrected state.
Claiming the soul before you,
His wages have now been paid.

As I stood there, the judge's gaze had changed.
The love in His eyes was so amazing,
My life will never be the same.

Drema R Taylor
March 01, 2023

DANCE WITH ME LORD

Dance with me Lord.
Hold me tight.
Spin me around in total delight.

The smile on Your face,
The love in Your eyes.
I'm lost in Your gaze, my heart cries out,
Lord! I love You.

As You hold me and spin me around,
The world fades away, I hear not a sound.
But my heart beats because of You.

Through the dance of my life,
I was amazed at the sights,
You were there all along the way,
Watching as I grew strong.

You made my life complete,
After I fell at Your feet,
Put my trust in You.

The dance paused, the music stopped,
You held me tight,
Life came to a halt,
When sorrow tore my heart.

DANCE WITH ME LORD

My spirit cried out, Lord! I need You.
As my life draws to an end,
Take me in Your arms again.

Dance with me, Lord, hold me tight.
Let me see the smile on Your face, the love in Your eyes,
As I cross over from death to life,
Never to see pain again.

Dance with me Lord.

Drema R Taylor
June 19, 2023

TEA PARTY FRIENDS

I've had tea parties before, with my teddy bears and friends,
For hours we sat and talked about all kinds of things.

We would marry princes, life would be so grand,
Living in castles, with pretty things in hand.

Ice cream for lunch and dinner every day,
Playing on swings and merry-go-rounds, laughing all the way.

Life was fun, so good, then darkness came,
Shattering our dreams, bringing sorrow and pain.

Gang wars entered our town, our neighborhood,
Peace vanished in a flash, guns blazing.

It rocked our world, never quite the same,
No more princes, no castles, no ice cream, all just a game.

Our dreams faded, innocence lost,
We cried in bed, mourning the cost.

The loss of a friend, and all we once knew,
In the wake of darkness, we grew.

My life has changed.
Nothing will ever be the same.

I met a very special friend.
He asked me to put my trust in Him.
The love that He gave me helped me know
I am loved and so adored,
That I can live with Him forevermore.

In my castle made by my King,
The Lord Jesus Christ is His name.
I'm going to a banquet with my special friend,
The Marriage Supper of the Lamb.

Drema R Taylor
June 21, 2023

IT'S BEEN A WHILE

I haven't heard from you lately,
We used to talk about everything,
Whatever concerned you greatly.

The passing of time, the things it brings.
I have called your name many times,
But you didn't hear a thing.

You kept going your own way,
Enduring pain along the way.

The path stretched out,
Seeming endless day by day.

I have watched as time has worn you down,
You're older now, living in your fears,
Crying all your tears, carrying wounds from those dear.

My heart breaks for you,
The hurts that have broken you apart,
Come back to me, fall into my arms,
Where you belong, dear heart.

Walk beside me, let me lead and guide,
Heal the hurt and pain that you have kept inside.

Let me comfort and console you,

Wrap my arms around you, bringing peace anew.

Drema R Taylor
July 17, 2023

THE STRUGGLE

Long known is the struggle of man,
Where it all started, where it all began.
The Garden of Eden, the perfect place,
No one could ask for more than this,
Paradise given to man.

So many scars, each with a story to tell,
Skinned knees and elbows, tears that came along,
The ones that get the band-aids,
And all the ones that are hidden all alone.

The tears of the soul so deep,
The hurts, the anguish, I know,
My heart crying out all alone.
No one sees, no one hears,
Here in the darkness of misery and tears.

The struggles of all the years.
My heart, my mind, screams out for help,
Does anyone hear? Does anyone care?

In misery and pain,
A voice came into the darkness of the deep.
I felt His love, His presence and peace.
As I listened, my heart raced,
I felt the warmth of His embrace.
My heart cried out to Him,
Please forgive me of my sin.

He gave me comfort and set me free,
Took the hurt and pain from me.
Now with Him, I'll live for all eternity.
He washed me clean in His blood and covered me in His love.

Drema R Taylor
July 10, 2023

SCARS

Scars run ugly and deep,
Scars of the heart, scars of the mind,
Scars on the skin, they hurt and bind.

You are skilled at hiding them away,
Smiling at faces you meet each day.
They don't know the real me.
They can't see the losses that weigh on me.

Past three days they don't care,
Get on with life they say.
They don't know it never goes away.

Ugly scars on His hands, His feet,
Borne by Him, for you and me.

Crown of thorns upon His head,
Blood streaming down, for us He bled.
A King so abused and hurt was He,
Dying on the cross to set us free.

The One who suffered greatly sought after me,
Showing love so pure, setting my spirit free.

He held me close to His breast,
Softly speaking into my heart,
He became my resting place.
The grief and hurts He took away.

He gave me peace within.

Don't let buried scars weigh you down,
For the Crowned One is always around,
Ready to set you free, for eternity.

Drema R Taylor
August 25, 2023

STANDING ON THE EDGE

The edge is a scary place to be,
One side is life, the other eternity.
Between now and the next breath you take,
You need to know for your own sake.

Where are you going? Where have you been?
Did you walk on the wild side of sin?
The things you have said, the things you have done,
Are you filled with dread? or have you won?

Each step you took, was it for good?
Or were you misunderstood?
Living on the edge, you don't even know you're there,
If you did, you would be so scared.

Death is at your door. Where will you live forevermore?
You are in the balance, a decision to be made.
Are you going to argue with God today?

The books have been opened. This is your life.
Are you going to confess or deny?
Time has brought you to your knees.
Are you scared to death or are you pleased?

As the Father looks over your life, will He find
The day and time you gave your life to Christ?
His blessed Son paid the price so you could live and not die.

Did you say yes, Lord? Or walk away in your sin,
  Never to know love or peace within?

Drema R Taylor
August 28, 2023

WISHING WELLS AND FAIRY TALES

Wishing wells have stories to tell,
Some with broken hearts,
Stand in front, tossing coins,
Seeking a fresh start.

Fresh starts are dreams to hold,
Broken hearts to mend.
Tears fall into the wells,
From pain that seems without end.

Disappointments abound,
In this place they gather,
Seeking mercy, grace,
For a life that is rather tattered.

A magic place to live in,
A better friend to find,
A better job, a better car,
A life so grand and kind.

Wishing wells and fairy tales
Do not reality make,
You can't change the past,
Or cover up your mistakes.

As heartbroken as you might be,
A crueler world awaits,
With flames and screams,

And cries for help, marking fate.

You might escape the here and now,
The sins you have committed,
The pain you have caused,
But your heart will still be broken, your life still in a mess,
And it will stay that way until you confess.

No more wishing wells,
No more fairy tales to tell,
The only story to be told,
Is of the King of glory to behold.

He stepped down from His throne,
To reclaim what is His own,
Gave His life to save your soul,
And set your spirit free, making you whole.

Call upon His name,
Find the power that saves,
And brings joy, peace, freedom,
Love, and self-control, until He calls you home.

Drema R Taylor
September 22, 2023

HEAVEN'S HEARTBEAT

The heartbeat of Heaven, a power that can shake
Its very foundation,
A power that can stir the core of your soul,
God's perfect salvation, a power to behold,
Beyond all imagination, a story of awe to be told.

Coming down through the ages.
The Commander of Angel Army's.
A warrior King has fought His battles against His enemies.
His heart not skipping a beat.

He burns in righteous indignation,
A mighty flame. A heat that is unquenchable.
He will defeat the one that tried to raise above and compete.

At the center of this heartbeat is Love,
Beginning without end,
Yet broken by guilt, sin, and shame.

The words that were spoken by Him,
Created the world and all that's within.
His love for His creation nailed Him to the tree that He created be.
Love held Him there for the world to see.

A love so pure, so willing to die,
To redeem His creation, you and I.

A price to be paid,
A sacrifice made,
Breath given away,
Father's heartbroken that day.

Sin is so dark and evil, not a spark of light within.
The payment due, the price was paid, a death so grim,
To the Love that created land and sea,
The heavens and all the galaxies.

Thought it worth His while, to come to earth as a child.
Live as a Man, feel our pain. To die so that we can live again.

Drema R Taylor
November 11, 2023

HEAVEN'S TIMEPIECE

Heaven has a timepiece,
It only has one hand.
It marks time as it goes by,
Forever and a day.

Forever is eternity, never the end to know,
A circle unbroken, its truth to show.

Eternity is fast approaching, just one breath away,
A day to reckon, coming without delay.
You may not have time to pray,
To find your path, to seek your way.

The hairs on your head are numbered.
Each day is passing by,
Your time is short as the seconds tick by.

You have questions to answer:
Are you known by Him?
Did you pass up the chance to say yes?
Did you walk right on by, not giving it a glance?

Good works are not in the picture, nowhere to be found.
All the good deeds you have done are dirt on the ground.

One last chance this might be, to save your soul,
And set you free, open your heart and your hands.

Accept the gift given to man.
Live in a castle with the King,
Cleansed, beloved, under His wing,
In the circle not made by man.

Drema R Taylor
September 12, 2023

EVIL'S PLAN

Evil comes in many shades,
Hidden so deep and dark,
Buried within the heart.
When it rears its ugly head,
Bad things happen,
Bad things said.

Such a sad, sorry state of affairs,
As a perfect life would have been theirs.
They had a Father who loved them much,
They would always feel His touch.

One day took a bad turn,
The woman crashed and burned.
She lost it all when she said yes,
I will try and taste instead,
I will know what it means to be like God,
Make my own plans.

The lovely creature that drew her in,
Was something far worse than sin.
Full of blackness and jealous desires,
Was he evil from the start?
Did it grow within his heart?

The couple lost their beautiful home,
They had to make it on their own.

Father's heart was hurting as He kicked them out of the garden,
The beautiful place He had made for them.

No more walks in the evening,
No more life of ease.
Toil and sweat for the rest of their days,
Heartbreak and sorrow as their family fell apart.

Envy and murder was just the start.
Grace and mercy entered in the day they committed sin.
No greater sacrifice was ever made,
Than the day the King of glory stepped onto the world stage.

To be born of a virgin,
The promise made, for His creation to save.
The pain and sorrow would be His,
For He had so much love to give.

From life to death to resurrected state,
To save His creation, it's not to late.
To know the one who sets you free,
And live throughout eternity.

With the one who paid your price,
And loved you with His life.

Drema R Taylor
September 18, 2023

ROBIN

There was a time and a place,
Where I saw your lovely face.
I heard your voice, oh so sweet,
Clear and ringing in my ear.

Your laughter, your smile,
Going the extra mile to help a friend in need,
Truly a friend indeed.

Loving, sweet, and kind,
You were a special child of mine.
My baby, my last one born,
Now my heart is torn, you are gone.

Hard to believe I won't see your face,
Or hear your voice again in this place.

Gone are the days we once shared,
Memories now take their place,
A picture in my mind brings a brighter time.

From your childhood to growing up,
How much I loved you, my sweetest love.

I miss you so, I always will,
You are my sweet baby girl still.

DANCE WITH ME LORD

You are in a place beyond my thinking,
An awesome place where peace, love, and joy abound,
And praises ring on high, angels in their heavenly choir.

The most powerful thing of all,
You have been redeemed by the Son of God,
Whose love for you is endless and sure.

One day I will join you there,
To sing Alleluias and Hosannas,
Keeping the praises ringing.

He greeted you there,
His promise to keep you safe,
Close to His breast forever.

I will see you soon, my dear child,
This place is not my home,
Just where I reside until He calls me home.

That joyous day, my soul was found.

Drema R Taylor
March 16, 2003

Made in the USA
Middletown, DE
14 February 2025